THE MERMAID LAGOON

AN EROTIC FAIRYTALE

VICTORIA RUSH

VOLUME 6

CLOVER'S FANTASY ADVENTURES -
BOOK 6

COPYRIGHT

For the uninhibited...

WANT TO AMP UP YOUR SEX LIFE?

Sign up for my newsletter to receive more free books and other steamy stuff. Discover a hundred different ways to wet your whistle!

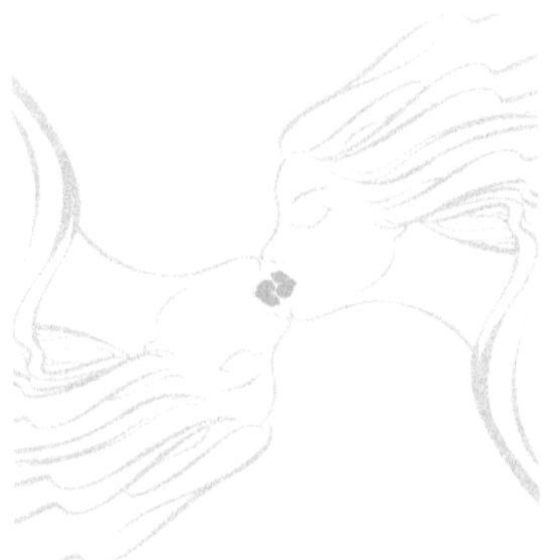

Victoria Rush Erotica

1

After the three explorers tumbled over the waterfall, they checked to make sure nothing was broken, then they continued downriver until they reached the coast. For the first couple of days, they foraged in the woods, eating wild game and chukruss and sleeping under the stars. The days were becoming longer and the nights warmer, and as they lay in their makeshift beds of pine boughs, they joked about their misadventure in the town of Longdale.

"That was a bit of an abrupt ending to our little adventure at the Cock and Hen bar," Jessop chuckled.

"It might have been amusing for *you*," Clover grunted, turning over to peer at him through thin eyelids. "But I assure you, almost being burned alive isn't an experience I'd like to revisit anytime soon."

"I think we'd best steer clear of witches and mages for a while," Tara nodded.

"At least ones who offer to give us special powers," Clover said.

"You don't miss your extra powers?" Jessop teased.

"It was fun seeing what it was like to be in a man's shoes for a little while," Clover smiled. "But having a penis is over-rated. I'm just as happy having my girly parts back, without all the extra mess."

"Except you make almost as much of a mess when you come as I do," Jessop snickered, adjusting his thickening tool remembering their threesome encounter at the brothel.

"At least I don't have to worry anymore about getting innocent farmgirls pregnant and having the whole town coming after me with pitchforks."

"Yeah," Tara chuckled. "I say we get as far away from that crazy place as possible."

"So where to now?" Jessop said. "You seem to know these parts better than anyone."

"We've strayed pretty far from where we first met up," Tara said. "With the days becoming warmer, why don't we head back north to see if we can find Clover's magic waterfall?"

Clover turned over on her bed of pine needles, propping her head on her elbow.

"I assume you're referring to the one that transported me here from my hometown, and not that last one that erased the mage's magic spell?"

"Yes," Tara nodded. "Aren't you still interested in returning to this strange place called Tennessee?"

"I suppose so. Although it'll never be half as exciting as staying with you two, where we seem to get into a new batch of trouble every place we go."

"Not by *design*, I assure you," Tara laughed. "You're the one always wanting to make friends with every new stranger we meet along the way."

"It's just that everything's so new and wonderful in this

strange land of Abbynthia. The witches, elves, and dragons remind me of my fairy tales from back home."

"You and your fairy tales," Tara huffed, standing up and slinging her quiver of arrows over her back. "Come on, let's head down to the shore and see if we can scare up some *seafood* for a change."

T he trio followed the rocky coastline north for a few miles and when it dipped down to a sandy cove, they followed a trail through the brush until it emerged onto the sheltered lagoon. Protected by tall cliffs on either side, it looked the perfect spot to set up camp and take a refreshing dip in the surf. But as they dipped their toes in the rolling waves, they heard a faint noise coming from behind a cluster of boulders near the side of the beach.

"Do you hear that?" Clover said, pausing to look at her friends.

Tara and Jessop stopped at the edge of the surf, turning their heads in the direction of the sound.

"Yes," Jessop nodded. "It sounds like a woman's voice."

"Like she's in *pain*," Tara said, pinching her eyebrows together.

"Let's see if she needs our help," Clover said, walking in the direction of the rocks.

"There you go again," Tara said, following close behind. "Always meddling in other people's business..."

"We can't just leave her there if she's in distress," Clover said, picking her way over the tumbled boulders.

But as they peered over the top of one of the rocks, they noticed a pretty girl with her head tilted back, moaning while she moved her hand between her legs under the foaming water.

"It doesn't look like she's in any *trouble* to me," Tara said. "Let's give her some privacy while she enjoys her moment alone. I don't think she needs any company at this particular moment."

As Tara tugged on Clover's arm, she resisted for a moment, gawking at the girl's naked figure. She had long, curly blonde hair, full lips, and an hourglass figure with perfectly tanned skin.

"It doesn't hurt to *watch* for a few moments," Clover grinned. "She's absolutely stunning."

"You're incorrigible," Tara said, easing up on her grip.

"And relentless," Jessop nodded, glancing at the pretty siren. "You'd think after getting almost lynched for your previous transgression, you'd want to steer clear of lonely blondes."

"Oh, come on," Clover said, grinning at her friend. "Tell me you wouldn't like a piece of that pretty ass too?"

"Time to go, you perverts," Tara said, grabbing Clover's and Jessop's arms, trying to pull them away. "Let's give this girl some peace..."

"Wait!" Clover whispered, her eyes suddenly bulging as the water began to recede from the girl's body. "Is that a–?"

"It's a *mermaid!*" Jessop nodded, his mouth dropping open. "I've heard stories about these creatures, but I've never seen one up close."

"It doesn't seem to have a..." Clover said, watching the girl's finned tail flapping excitedly in the surf as she grew progressively more aroused. "And yet she's touching herself like she's–"

"Every living creature has sex in *one* form or another," Tara nodded. "How do you think they reproduce?"

"I have *no* idea" Clover said, staring at the beautiful girl while she twisted and groaned in pleasure. "But I'd sure as hell love to learn how. She's way sexier than in any of the stories I've read..."

"Leave the poor girl alone," Tara said, tugging on Clover's and Jessop's arms more firmly to pull them away. "She's obviously chosen this secluded location for a reason. Put your dicks back in your pants and let her enjoy her moment of solitude..."

As Tara pulled on her friends' arms, the sudden movement attracted the attention of the mermaid lying on the beach, and she suddenly turned her face in their direction.

"What the...?" she grunted, quickly sliding her body into the surf and starting to swim away.

"Wait!" Clover said, jumping up and waving her arms over her head. "We don't mean you any harm! We're here alone just looking for food. Can we talk with you for a moment?"

The mermaid paused for a moment, peering up at the pretty redhead. There was something unusual about her that she found intriguing, and not yet noticing her two other friends still hiding behind the rocks, she swam slowly up to the side of the boulder, peering over the edge with wide eyes.

Clover picked her way down over the rocks and stopped about ten feet away to indicate she wasn't any threat.

"Who are you?" she said, peering at the girl's half-submerged face.

"My name's Lorelei," the mermaid said, raising up slowly. "But my friend's call me Lori."

"You speak *English*?" Clover said, hardly believing her luck stumbling upon the captivating sea creature.

"I was separated from my tribe when I was young," the

girl nodded. "And raised by a gentle widow who cared for me until I was old enough to return to my home."

"Where's that?" Clover said, peering along the coastline for any sign of civilization.

"A few miles offshore on a remote island called Crescent Key. It's an atoll really, ringed by a large coral reef..."

"Do *other* mermaids live there?" Clover said, squinting her eyes trying to find any sign of land out to sea.

"There's a group of a hundred or so of us there," the girl nodded. "Mermaids and mermen. We don't come to the mainland very often. Usually only to collect fruit and other necessary provisions. The soil on our island isn't very conducive to growing crops–"

Suddenly the girl glanced upward, noticing Tara and Jessop making their way down in their direction.

"I should be going now..." the girl said, pushing away from the rock.

"Wait, these are my friends," Clover said, holding up her hand to keep the girl from swimming away. "We would never harm you in any way. We just noticed you were alone, and wondered if you needed any help..."

"No," the girl said, darting her eyes between Clover and her approaching friends. "I was just–"

"This is Tara and Jessop," Clover said, introducing her friends as they approached the floating mermaid. "And this is Lorelei, I mean *Lori*..."

"Hello," Tara said, smiling at the girl warmly. "We didn't mean to disturb you. My friend Clover can sometimes be a little presumptuous–"

"Are you an *elf*?" the mermaid said, noticing Tara's pointed ears. "I've never seen one of those before."

"And I've never seen a *mermaid* before," Tara chuckled.

"Me neither," Jessop said, staring at the sexy sea creature with wide eyes.

"You all look so different," the mermaid said, beginning to relax her body while floating upside down as she scanned the faces and figures of the unlikely trio. "How did you manage to come together?"

"Quite by accident," Tara chuckled. "Much like we found you. We were all running away from something, and we seemed to form a common bond. How about you? Are you here alone? Where are you from?"

"I live on an offshore island with my small band of fellow mermaids and mermen–"

"*Mermen*?" Tara said. "Are they as beautiful as you? Because if so, I'd love to meet some of your friends..."

"We don't stray from the island very often," Lori chuckled. "But if I don't return soon, they'll probably send a search party out looking for me."

"Would you like to stay a little longer?" Clover said, eager to learn more about the girl's life as a mermaid. "We were going to catch some fish and prepare a fire. That is, if you *eat* fish–"

"Yes, of course," Lori smiled. "All we have on our little island is some coconuts and breadfruit. We're creatures of the sea after all. But I have to admit that I haven't had a *cooked* fish for a while..."

"It's decided then," Clover said, resting her arm against the rock. "Would you like to help us catch something big enough for all of us to eat? Maybe you can steer a snapper or a grouper into the shallow water and we can spear it with our arrows."

"That's a novel way to catch fish," Lori chuckled. "I thought you humans like to use hooks with bait?"

"We're a bit short of that right now," Tara said. "We lost

most of our supplies when we fell over a waterfall a few days ago..."

"How did *that* happen?" Lori said, peering up at her new friends with a lopsided smile.

"I guess we're not quite as good a swimmer as you are," Tara laughed. "We'll tell you all about it around the fire."

"As long as you're not planning to cook up anything larger than a grouper..."

"We wouldn't dream of it," Clover murmured, peering down at Lori's curved backside as she flipped over to round up some dinner. "Although I can think of a few *other* ways I'd like to eat you up..."

2

———

After Lori helped the three friends corner and capture a large snapper in the lagoon, Tara filleted the fish while Jessop built a fire on the beach. As they all sat down around the fire using skewers to cook the meat, Lori peered around the group and smiled.

"I haven't had grilled snapper since my noni raised me as a child. It tastes so much better smoked over a fire."

"Your people haven't learned how to make fire?" Clover said.

"We rarely have any need, since we spend most of our time in the sea."

Clover paused for a moment, examining Lori's mermaid figure.

"It seems so unusual, seeing someone with a half-human, half-fish body," she said.

"I can imagine," Lori chuckled. "But it's just as strange for us seeing humans walking upright with two legs."

Tara peered at the girl, wondering why she was alone.

"Is your small band on the island the only group of mermaids you're aware of?" she asked.

"Yes," Lori nodded. "We have no idea how we managed to evolve into our unusual shape."

"Maybe it was one of those crazy witches like we met in the forest," Jessop chuckled, having a hard time keeping his eyes from straying lower to stare at the girl's exposed breasts.

"Or maybe it was a random coupling between a human and a porpoise or some other sea creature," Lori smiled, noticing the bulge in his pants.

"If you don't mind my asking," Clover said, reflecting on how they first discovered her. "How do you mermaids reproduce? Unlike we humans, your sexual organs appear to be hidden..."

"We have slits on the underside of our bellies, just like dolphins and whales. When aroused, mermens' penises protrude from their slits and we copulate in much the same manner I imagine you humans do."

"Does it feel good, like it does for us?" Clover asked.

"Of course," Lori smiled. "Sexual play is a big part of our culture. We don't just have sex to procreate."

"So it would seem," Jessop said, running his eyes unabashedly over the mermaid's curvy figure.

"Jessop!" Tara scolded, furrowing her brow in disapproval at her friend's ill-mannered comment.

"It's quite alright," Lori laughed, returning Jessop's stare as she inspected his athletic figure. "For us merfolk, sex is a perfectly natural and fun activity. I'm just sorry I wasn't the one who caught *you* having sex first–"

Suddenly the group's attention was diverted by the sound of two mermen splashing ashore as they crawled up the beach on their hands and knees like half-human walruses.

"Lorelei!" the larger one said with a stern gaze. "You know you're not allowed to fraternize with humans."

"It's okay," Lori said. "These are my friends. We met while I was...collecting chukruss."

"There's no such thing as *friendly* humans," the merman said, noticing Jessop reaching for his sword reflexively.

"Please," Tara said, motioning for Jessop to stand down. "We mean you no harm. Why don't you join us? There's plenty of food for everyone."

The mermen peered at the three humans suspiciously, although Tara noticed they lingered a little longer examining the figures of the two women. The larger of the two was quite handsome, with long black hair, powerful arms, and a fur-covered chest.

"It's okay, Ronan," Lori said, patting the sand between her and Tara. "Come see what it's like to eat cooked fish for a change. These people aren't like most humans."

As the mermen slowly crawled up to join the group, Lori introduced them as Ronan and Caol, then the three friends introduced themselves in turn. Tara handed each of them a skewer of grilled snapper from the fire, and they flinched when they brought the hot flesh on their lips.

"You might want to let it cool for a moment before eating it," Tara chuckled, passing them a chopped chukruss. "It tastes even better with a bit of citrus juice sprinkled on top."

She squeezed the other half of the fruit overtop of her skewer, then the mermen copied her lead, biting into the snapper hesitatingly. They peered at one another with raised eyebrows, then quickly devoured the fish while Tara prepared another skewer.

"What do you think?" Tara said, handing the mermen a second serving.

"It's different from what we're used to," Ronan said, downing the fish hungrily.

"Different can be good," Tara smiled, glancing at the mermen's hairy chests and curvy hips.

"Sometimes," Ronan nodded, peering over his thick brow while he examined the girls' figures.

"Lori tells us you have a small colony offshore," Clover said, trying to ease the sexual tension among the group.

Ronan turned his head to glare at Lori disapprovingly.

"You know you're not supposed to tell anyone where we live."

"I'm sorry," Lori said. "They were just curious where I came from, and we've been getting to know one another while we shared a meal together."

"And what do we know about *them*?" Caol interjected, seeming more concerned about Jessop and his gleaming weapon by his side than the pretty girls distracting Ronan. "How do we know they're not part of a larger group wanting to attack us?"

"I assure you that we're alone," Tara said. "We're just as wary of other people as you are. We've had more than our fair share of run-ins with nefarious humans as well."

"Where do you come from?" Ronan said, peering at Clover's red hair, Tara's pointed ears, and Jessop's fair skin. "You all look so different."

"Jessop's home is in the Norseland, and I come from Abbynthia," Tara said. "Clover comes from some place none of us have ever heard of."

"Somewhere where mermaids and mermen only live in *fairy tales*," Clover laughed.

"Fairy tales?" Lori said, looking at Clover with a puzzled expression.

"They're make-believe stories where all the strange creatures and characters are made up."

"Except these ones aren't *make-believe*," Tara smiled, staring at the mermens' handsome faces and curvy asses.

"Perhaps you'd like to come visit our island sometime," Lori said, recognizing everyone's growing attraction with one another.

"How would we get there?" Clover said. "We don't have a boat, and we surely couldn't swim that far."

"I'm sure Ronan and Caol wouldn't mind carrying you on their *backs*, would you boys?" Lori smiled.

"I don't know," Ronan said, surprised by Lori's unexpected invitation. "It's one thing to be friendly with humans on their own soil, but it's quite another to reveal our hiding spot."

"Don't you think they would have already taken advantage of us already if they meant us any harm?" Lori said, tapping her fingers over the tips of Tara's pointed arrows. "With their advanced weapons, they could have easily overpowered us while we were out of our element. Besides, maybe they can teach us how to make our *own* fires and cook fish as delicious as this..."

Ronan paused for a moment, then turned to his fellow tribesman.

"What do you think, Caol?"

"There's a hundred of us and only three of them," Caol nodded, his pupils widening as he peered at Jessop more warmly. "Plus, they'd be on our turf, far from the mainland."

"Maybe just for a day or two then," Ronan said, peering up at the sun angling slowly westward. "This fire could prove useful to us in other ways..."

"What do you say, guys?" Clover said, peering at her friends excitedly. "Are you up for another adventure?"

"I don't know where you get this wanderlust from," Tara said, turning to Jessop for his input. "I think you've read too many fairy tales with happy endings."

"We could use a *happy ending* for a change," Jessop said, staring at Lori's bare breasts. "I'm game if you are."

3

———————

"Alright," Tara nodded. "Jessop should go with one of the mermen since he's heavier than us girls." She glanced over at Ronan and smiled. "I'll hitch a ride with Ronan, and Clover can go with Lori. Are you sure you can carry us all that way out to sea?"

"You'll have to wrap your legs around my hips and hold onto my hair for support," Ronan nodded. "It'll be a bit of a bumpy ride."

"That's quite alright," Tara smiled. "I'm getting used to bumpy rides."

After the trio collected their gear, Lori and the mermen crawled down to the edge of the shore, lowering torsos into the surf while raising their midsections out of the water to allow their new friends to climb on top.

The two girls couldn't help noticing that the section of their bodies where their human and fish parts merged was shaped distinctly like a human ass, even though it was covered in fish scales. As they rested on their midsections and wrapped their legs around their torsos, the girls' pussies tingled in excitement as they reached down to grasp their partners' flowing locks for extra support. Even Jessop seemed momentarily distracted as he sat atop Caol's muscular rump, adjusting his package while he ran his hands over his rippling back.

As Lori and the mermen began to swim into deeper water, their bodies undulated over the surface like dolphins swimming beside a ship. While Clover and her friends held on for dear life, the creatures glided effortlessly through the sea, dipping their heads in and out of the water as they spouted spray to catch their breath after every new dip.

Clover leaned forward to wrap her arms around Lori's chest, copping a feel of her firm breasts whenever her body shifted atop her back. She glanced over at Tara, noticing her riding Ronan's bare back like a cowgirl as she ground her pussy into his flexing hips while he undulated up and down through the churning waves. Glancing a few feet further to the side, she saw Jessop's cock hardening under his tight trousers as he pulled on Caol's flowing hair while humping his ass.

"This is insane!" Clover shouted to her friends, feeling more alive than she had in years. "This is way better than taking a *boat!*"

"No kidding," Tara grunted, tilting her pussy directly over Ronan's flexing buttocks. "This is the best sex I've had in ages!"

Clover peered over at Jessop, who was bumping up and down over Caol's ass.

"How are you doing over there, Jessop?" she shouted.

"Good," he panted as he tightened his legs around Caol's flexing hips. "I just hope he doesn't buck me off before we get there."

Clover glanced down at Caol's face, noticing a sly smile on his face. Whether he was enjoying having Jessop at his mercy in his own element, or he was becoming equally excited having a human humping his ass while he swam through the surf, she couldn't be sure. But one thing seemed certain. This likely wouldn't be the *last* time the three of them had a bumpy ride with their new hosts.

After a couple of hours riding on their backs, a mound of green suddenly appeared on the horizon, and as they got closer, they saw a small island surrounded by a coral reef. While the waves began to break over the outer barrier, Ronan, Lori, and Caol slowed their pace, winding through a narrow gap in the glittering coral into a tranquil, turquoise-colored lagoon.

The three hosts swam up to the beach on the small central island, and as Clover, Tara, and Jessop tumbled off, shaking out their cramping leg muscles, they turned around to peer at the incredible beauty of the lagoon. Completely surrounded by a rainbow-colored reef, the basin was filled with a profusion of striped fish, spotted rays, and scores of mermaids swimming through the crystal-clear water while the overhead sun shimmered over the reflection from the white sandy floor.

"Holy cow," Clover said, dipping her toes into the warm, shallow water. "This is even more beautiful than I dreamed. I'm going to write my very own fairy tale story when I get back home."

"Just make sure you tell it as a *fairy tale*," Tara smiled as Ronan peered back at her, floating gently on his back a few meters offshore. "Because if any other humans ever found this paradise, they'd surely make short work of it."

She squinted her eyes through the shimmering water, noticing something large and pink protruding from his belly, and she gasped when she realized it was his erect penis, shaped like a giant curved slug. Far from being repulsed by it, she felt her pussy still throbbing from the pounding she'd received on the long trip over from the mainland.

"Come in and enjoy the water," Lori smiled, flapping her tail playfully next to him. "It's even more beautiful *underneath*. You've never seen so many colorful fish as you'll find here."

As the three friends waded into the shallow water of the lagoon, a school of baby sea lions suddenly swirled up around them, wanting to play. When they dipped their bodies below the surface, the animals swam up surprisingly close, peering at their human faces with their cute puppy dog eyes. While the pups flapped and rolled in the bubbling surf, Clover, Tara, and Jessop mimicked their movement, trying to keep up. As they smiled and reached out trying to touch the playful creatures, their eyes widened watching the menagerie of fish swimming idly by like nothing was happening.

Clover had never seen such placid and beautiful sea creatures her whole life, and the sun had started to set by the time she and her friends finally dragged themselves out of the water, completely exhausted.

"Oh my God," Clover gasped, flopping onto the shore as she stared up at the wispy clouds passing overhead. "I never want to leave this place. It's got everything anybody could ever want. Abundant sea life, fresh water, a protected offshore lagoon–"

"Hot mermaids and mermen..." Tara grunted, slumping down beside her.

"Did you see what *I* saw?" Clover said, turning her head to grin at her friend. "Ronan's big, fleshy dick? I think he kind of fancies you. He never seemed to stray far from your side the whole time we were in there."

"Yeah, I noticed," Tara said. "It's shaped a bit strange, but I could definitely go for a ride on his *other* side anytime he wants."

"Whatever happened to giving these sea creatures their privacy and not leering at them when they're sexually aroused?" Jessop said, pulling his sagging pants up over his hips.

"That was before we went for a bumpy ride on their beautiful asses," Tara grinned, glancing at his still-tumescent tool in his wet trousers. "Speaking of which, I noticed you didn't seem to mind too much either."

"Oh *that?*" Jessop said, peering down at the bulge in his pants. "That's just from watching all these pretty mermaids swimming around completely naked. *Anybody* would get hard under those circumstances."

"Um-hmm," Clover teased. "Are you sure you weren't getting excited about putting that tool somewhere *else*?"

"I wouldn't even know where to put it," Jessop said. "Unlike *you* two, who have a giant *worm* to latch onto whenever the mood strikes."

"And the mood is definitely *striking*," Tara said, peering out at the swirling band of mermaids and mermen mating unabashedly in the clear water of the lagoon.

"I'm growing an appetite for something else," Clover said, feeling her stomach starting to grumble. "I've worked up quite a hunger playing with those cute sea lions. I wonder if our new friends would be interested in helping us scare up some more food."

Tara stood up and peered out into the lagoon, noticing Ronan and Lori gliding idly nearby.

"Are you guys getting hungry again?" she said. "What have you got to eat around here?"

Lori swam up to the water's edge, resting her breasts in the sand as her tail flapped softly in the water behind her.

"We typically feed on smaller fish found in the lagoon. But you'll also find coconuts and breadfruit on the trees further inland."

Ronan swam up beside her, resting on his muscular haunches.

"Would you like us to round up some larger fish, like you had by the shore?" he said, flexing his buttocks against the pliant sand.

"That would be lovely," Tara said, imagining it was *her* lying beneath him while he penetrated her with his large fleshy organ.

"Can you wait until we come back before you start another fire?" he nodded. "We'd like you to teach us how you do it so we can make one for ourselves."

"Of course," Tara smiled. "I'll be ready whenever you are."

"I *bet* you will," Clover chuckled as Ronan headed toward the exit of the lagoon with a group of other mermen.

Lori grinned, overhearing the two girls' conversation.

"If you'd like to collect some coconuts and breadfruit," she said. "We mermaids can help you prepare the side dishes."

"Of course," Clover nodded, heading into the lush foliage in the center of the island with Tara and Jessop.

When they returned with an armful of husks from the trees, a group of mermaids with stone axes began splitting the fruit and chopping them up into bite-sized pieces. Fifteen minutes later, the friends saw a commotion near the small opening of the lagoon, and soon after a large blue-skinned fish began circling in the shallow water as twenty mermen cornered it, forcing it into the shallow water. When the creature slowed by the side of the beach, one of the mermaids reared up with a large club, striking it hard over the head, making it fall limp.

"That's one way to kill a fish," Jessop chuckled as the men hauled the huge fish onto the beach and the women began slicing it open with sharpened stone knives.

"How do you humans usually do it?" Ronan said, crawling up beside Tara and Clover who were preparing the firepit.

"We normally slice off its head with a knife or some other sharp object."

"That might work with a *smaller* fish, but we don't have a knife as big as yours to slice off its head. By the time we finished hacking it off with our stone tools, the poor creature would die a slow death. At least this way is fast and merciful."

"That's a mighty big fish you caught," Tara said, trying to change the subject. "Do you normally eat your fish raw?"

"Like all the other fish in the sea, yes," Ronan nodded. "I guess we haven't yet learned how to use our human parts quite so creatively as you."

"I'm not so sure we're as different as you might think," Tara smiled. "Crowd around while we show you one of our neatest tricks. But I have to warn you, fire can be both a blessing and a curse. If you're not careful, it will burn your entire island down to the dirt."

"Is that why you place rocks around it to keep it from spreading?" Ronan said, noticing the ring of stones the girls had placed in the center of the beach.

"Yes, although it's not quite as important here in the middle of the sand as it is in the forest. In this case, the rocks are here more to facilitate the *cooking* process than anything else."

"So how do you make the fire?" he asked.

"Through *friction*," Tara said, placing a dry piece of driftwood inside the perimeter of stones. "By rubbing combustible materials together until they generate enough heat to spark a fire. Let me show you."

Tara twisted her knife upright overtop of the flat driftwood until it made a small hollow. Then she placed a long, straight twig with a beveled end against the string of her bow, turning it a hundred-and-eighty degrees to twist the bowstring around the shaft. As Clover held a small rock over the top of the stick, Tara placed the beveled end into the hollow on the board, swiping her bow forward and back. As the stick began rotating rapidly in the shallow depression, within a matter of seconds some smoke began drifting up from the dry wood.

Jessop leaned down to place some crumpled leaves against the base of the twig, then he blew softly into the smoking hollow until a small flame erupted around the shaft. As he piled larger twigs and driftwood onto the flame, before long a large fire erupted in the pit, supported with larger logs.

"That's pretty impressive," Ronan said, nodding his head. "But how do I make the *bow*?"

Tara turned toward the handsome merman, examining his powerful physique in the light of the flickering flame.

"If you'll let us stay the night, I can show you that *tomorrow*," she smiled. "That takes a little longer. If you're a good boy, I might even show you how to fling arrows with it. You never know when you might need it to defend yourself against less harmless humans."

"Oh, I'll be a good boy," he grinned, peering at Tara's pointed ears and plump breasts pushed up against her wet smock. "But something tells me you're not quite as harmless as you let on."

4

After everyone enjoyed a delicious dinner of seared tuna and roasted breadfruit, the group assembled around the fire to listen to stories about their adventures on opposite sides of the world. Everyone seemed especially interested to hear about Clover's life in the strange land of Tennessee, where people rode around in mechanized vehicles and watched moving pictures for entertainment. But as the fire began to dim, the three friends' thoughts began to turn to other matters.

"Where do you merfolk usually sleep?" Tara said, peering at Ronan. "I mean, you're half fish and half human. Do you sleep in the water or on land?"

"It depends what kind of mood we're in," he smiled. "Sometimes we like to sleep in the sheltered water of the lagoon, and sometimes we sleep in special hammocks we've fashioned between the trees."

"That sounds a little more comfortable than sleeping on pine needles or scratchy sand," Tara chuckled. "Have you got extra room for three weary travelers?"

"I think we can squeeze you in," he said. "Come, let's get you situated."

As Ronan, Lori, and Caol led each of the three friends separately to a different section of the island, they peered up at the tall coconut trees growing adjacent to one another. Hanging between each pair lay a long hammock, swaying gently in the evening breeze.

"Wow," Tara said to Ronan, admiring the workmanship of the sturdy swings. "How do you manufacture these things? It looks as hardy as anything we make out of cloth."

"We weave the material using cross-patterns of coconut leaves," he said. "It can be surprising strong when woven in the correct manner."

"And these *ropes* holding them onto the trees?" she said, pushing her hands down firmly onto the soft matting. Are they strong enough to support your weight?"

"The cords are made in much the same way," he nodded. "We braid and twine them into separate strands. The fibers within the plants are remarkably strong when pulled end-to-end."

Ronan picked up a palm frond that had fallen from one of the trees and tore off a long leaf, placing one end in Tara's hands.

"Here, see for yourself," he said. "Pull your end as hard as you can while I hold the other."

Tara pulled on the leaf firmly while she watched Ronan's chest and arm muscles flexing to hold the other end.

"I see what you mean," she nodded, feeling a dampness building up between her legs. "But is it strong enough to support *two* people?"

"That could be arranged–" Ronan smiled, tilting his head.

Tara leaned forward to kiss him, and he placed his arms around her shoulders, returning the gesture. Within seconds, the two of them were pressing their tongues into each other mouths, panting heavily.

"Why don't we get off this sand, where we can explore each other's bodies more comfortably?" Tara said.

Ronan scooped her up in his arms and placed her into the hammock, then he pulled himself up onto the swing, resting gently on top of her. As they began kissing again, she felt his hardening cock pressing against her hips, and she pulled away to smile at him in the moonlight.

"This isn't fair, you being all *naked* and everything. Let me take off my human clothes so we can feel each other more naturally."

Ronan tilted over onto his side, and she sat up in the hammock, pulling off her tight sheepskin suit, throwing it onto the ground. As she turned back toward him, she noticed his swelling organ had grown to twelve inches, glistening and writhing like an enormous undulating tongue.

"You're built differently than the other men I've known," Tara said, pulling her head closer to inspect his tool more carefully. "May I touch it?"

"Absolutely," Ronan smiled.

As she placed her hands around his phallus, it twitched in her palms, and she noticed a drop of dew spilling out of the tip.

"It feels magnificent," Tara said, her eyes bulging in wonder. "Does it feel good when I touch it?"

"Of course," Ronan panted. "I like the way you're touching it..."

Tara couldn't resist leaning further down to inspect it, and as she smelled his musk, she pressed her tongue against the organ, tasting his juice. It tasted both sweet and salty, and before long, she was lapping his dripping cock like an ice cream cone.

"Does it feel even better when I touch it with my *tongue*?" she smiled.

"Mmm, yes," Ronan grunted, pressing his head back against the hammock.

"Do your mermaid girlfriends touch you like this sometimes?"

"Yes, but somehow it's more exciting when you do it."

Although his erection was too large for Tara to get her mouth all the way around it, she teased him while licking the whole length of it up and down. Noticing he grunted louder the closer she moved toward the tip, she began circling the flared end while gripping his scaly hips with her hands. Before long, Ronan began rocking his hips more forcefully toward her face, and when he reached out to hold her head as he grunted loudly, Tara raised up.

"Why did you *stop*?" he panted, peering at her on the verge of climax.

"If you're like *most* men I've known," she grinned. "You won't be much use to me after you come. I want to enjoy this piece of flesh while you're still hard and in the mood."

Tara raised herself onto her knees and straddled Ronan's hips with her thighs, then she angled her wet pussy toward his throbbing tool, slowly taking his tip into her slit.

"It's so warm," Tara moaned, surprised by how natural it felt sliding into her pussy.

"And *hard*..." Ronan grunted, trying to push his organ deeper inside her.

"Whoa, boy," Tara said, placing her hands on his hairy chest for support. "Not so fast. I'm not built the same way as your mermaid girls. The men where I come from are a lot smaller than you."

"You don't think you can take *all* of me?" Ronan said, squeezing Tara's breasts with his webbed hands.

"I think so," Tara nodded, pressing her hips slowly down over his enormous cock. "If I can push a *baby* through this canal, I'm pretty sure I can fit your monster. Just give me a minute to ease it in..."

As she twisted and rocked her hips slowly over his midsection, Ronan's tool sunk deeper and deeper inside her until her vulva pressed against his scaly skin. It felt unusual feeling his rough skin against her sensitive flesh, but as she began to rock her hips forward and back, the sensation of her hard clit sliding over his scaly bumps just added to her excitement.

"Mmm," she purred, leaning forward to press her breasts against his hairy chest. "That feels better. Now *fuck* me with that huge dagger of yours. You are one hot animal."

"Oh yeah?" Ronan smiled, grabbing the sides of Tara's head and kissing her passionately while humping his hips hard against her pussy. "Do you like getting fucked by a fish for change?"

"I'd hardly call you a *fish*," Tara grunted. "More like a whale. That prick of yours is unlike anything I've ever tried."

"How many have you tried exactly?" Ronan grinned.

"Probably not as many *girls* as you've had," Tara said, angling her head toward the beach. "I saw you sampling some of the ladies in the lagoon. How do you like fucking a *human* woman for a change?"

"It's definitely strange having your legs spread apart while we copulate," he grunted, playing with Tara's breasts. "But you're not so different from the other girls."

"Oh no?" Tara said, squeezing Ronan's tool with her pussy while she pretended to pout. "Not even a little tighter? Or *prettier*...?"

"You have your charms, that's for sure," he said, caressing her pointed ears. "And you're very beautiful–"

Tara sat upright so she could watch Ronan's face.

"Shut up and fuck me," she said. "I want to feel you squirting inside me when you come. Do you ejaculate like other men?"

"If by *ejaculate*, you mean deposit my seed inside my partner, yes," he groaned.

"Good," Tara said, grabbing hold of his chest hairs as she humped his dick more forcefully. "Because right now, all I can think about is spouting little mermaids, or mer-elves, or whatever strange offspring we'd produce."

Ronan smiled as he watched Tara's bobbing breasts while she rocked her body atop the swaying swing.

"I've never had a female take charge like you do," he grunted, squeezing her more firmly.

"The mermaids don't like to be on top sometimes?" Tara grinned.

"There's not really a top or bottom when you're swimming in the water," he groaned. "It's mostly just a bunch of rolling around..."

"That sounds like fun. Perhaps we can try that tomorrow."

"My pleasure," Ronan said. "As long as the other girls don't get jealous."

"I'm sure we can find a way to share the spoils."

"You mean...?"

"Absolutely," Tara grinned. "You don't think we invited Lori to join us on the beach just because we wanted to share some *food* with her?"

"You're full of surprises," Ronan grunted, flipping Tara over onto her back as he pounded her harder with his slippery instrument.

As she peered up into his grimacing face, suddenly she felt an explosion of fluid jetting out of her pussy while she gripped his flexing hips with her legs.

"Yes, baby," she gasped, feeling her pussy contracting tightly around his spasming tool. "Come for me. Let's make lots of little tadpoles."

5

———

On the other side of the island, Clover and Lori had made similar sleeping arrangements, deciding to share a cot instead of bunking in separate swings further apart.

"I've wanted to lie with you ever since I saw you touching yourself behind the rock in the lagoon," Clover confessed, cuddling up next to the mermaid on the surprisingly comfortable hammock.

"Same here," Lori grinned, kissing Clover gently on her lips. "You looked so cute trying to hide while you spied on me."

"You mean you saw me the whole time?" Clover's eyes flared.

"Pretty much. I was hoping to entice you down closer to the water..."

"So you could steal me away to your secluded island and have your way with me?"

"Something like that," Lori said, rolling overtop of Clover and rubbing their hips together.

"I wouldn't even know where to start–" Clover said.

"Let me take care of that," Lori said, wiggling down lower over Clover's naked stomach. "You're a bit more of an open book..."

As she nibbled her way toward Clover's crotch, Clover spread her legs far apart, raising her knees to give Lori freer access.

"You're so *soft* around your sex," Lori said, rolling her cheeks over Clover's furry mound. "Do all humans have hair on their genitals?"

"In this world, yes," Clover chuckled. "But where I come from, most women shave themselves down there to make everything nice and smooth."

"I like it this way," Lori said, pressing her nose into Clover's muff and smelling her scent. "It reminds me of the merman's hairy chests. It's very sexy."

"Don't you have sex with the *mermaids* also? I thought you said your tribe was very open and playful about your sexual practices..."

Lori smiled as she lowered her lips onto Clover's glistening vulva.

"Of course. But you're far more interesting than the other women. Everything is so much easier to reach and stimulate with you."

"Mmm," Clover purred, twisting her hips as Lori probed her slit with her tongue. "I like the feeling of your lips on my pussy."

"It's strange to see all your reproductive parts on the outside of your body," Lori said, lapping her tongue up and down the sides of Clover's dripping lips.

"They're not *all* on the outside," Clover smiled. "Most of the baby-making stuff is on the inside. Only the parts that feel good are on the outside."

"Hmm," Lori said, lapping Clover's pussy like a puppy

dog, savoring her secretions while she swallowed Clover's juices. "Do you like the way I'm stimulating you?"

"Yes," Clover groaned. "But there's a special spot at the top of my folds that feels even better. Let me show you..."

Clover reached down to hold Lori's head gently, then she directed her up a few inches until the mermaid's lips encircled her clit.

"There," she grunted. "Can you feel that little bump?"

"Yes," Lori said. "But it's not much bigger than a breadfruit seed. Is *this* where you derive all your pleasure?"

"Not all of it," Clover moaned. "But it's a good place to start. Roll your tongue over it and suck it gently between your lips..."

Lori did as Clover instructed, and as Clover felt her pleasure beginning to rise, she ran her fingers through Lori's golden hair, gyrating her hips against her glistening face.

"Yes, baby," Clover panted. "Just like that. You're going to make me come if you keep doing it that way–"

"Come?" Lori said, bobbing her head up with pinched eyebrows.

"It means to climax or reach the peak of my pleasure. Don't stop, I'm almost there..."

Lori lowered her head back down and placed her hands around Clover's flexing buttocks, pulling her pussy harder toward her face. The harder she sucked on Clover's nub, the louder she groaned, and as she began to raise her ass above the hammock's matting, suddenly she jetted a hard stream of fluid onto Lori's face. The mermaid paused for a moment, temporarily taken aback, then she planted her face back between Clover's thighs, enjoying the impromptu shower. When Clover finished shaking in her arms, Lori squiggled up next to her, gently kissing her on her lips.

"How did I do for my first time with a human?" she asked.

"You're a natural," Clover smiled, kissing Lori passionately as she rolled over to press her hips against the mermaid. "I only hope I can be half as skilled making you feel good."

"You already have," Lori smiled, slipping her hands through Clover's auburn locks. "You and your friends have been an unexpected pleasure for me and the rest of our tribe. I'm so glad Ronan and Caol agreed to let you come to our lagoon."

"I think Ronan had similar designs on Tara," Clover smiled. "And Caol and Jessop seem to be showing more than a passing interest in each other, despite all their macho posturing."

"Yes," Lori chuckled. "Something tells me they'll be learning just as much about one another's sexual preferences right now as we are."

"Speaking of," Clover said, twisting Lori's nipples gently between her fingertips. "Can you teach me how to please you like I did with you? You're a little more mysterious, with all your interesting parts hidden beneath the surface..."

"Not all of them," Lori smiled, squeezing Clover's tits as she played with her nipples. "We're not so different from you. We've got a slit just like you for inserting our mate's genitals, and some sensitive parts around the opening to make it feel good."

"Can you show me?" Clover said. "I want to learn how to be as good a lover as your fellow mermen and mermaids."

"If you insist," Lori said, flopping onto her back as she curled her tail up playfully. "My opening is in roughly the same place..."

Clover ran her hands down over Lori's midsection,

feeling her flesh slowly transition from smooth skin to bumpy scales. As she swiped the sides of her curvy flanks, she noticed a small opening in the center of her hips, gently puckering and emitting little bubbles.

"Huh!" Clover gasped. "Is that–?"

"Yes," Lori said, tilting her head up to watch Clover caressing her. "Press your finger inside me. I'm already wet from touching you earlier."

Clover raised up on her knees and straddled Lori's hips, sliding her right hand gently over the flaring hole. When she felt how slippery the fluid around the opening was, she smiled and pressed her index finger slowly inside.

"You're not going to chomp it off or anything, like an octopus or a moray eel?"

"Not until you finish with me," Lori grinned. "You feel far too good right now to gobble up."

Clover smiled, pressing her finger deeper into the mermaid's cavity.

"Do you have a special sensitive spot, like me?" Clover said, feeling around the labyrinthine folds in her pussy.

"Yes," Lori said, rolling her hips sensuously as Clover probed her. "On the upper surface, close to the opening, you'll feel a bulge..."

Clover turned her finger and curled it upward then her eyes suddenly widened.

"I feel something," she nodded. "But it's a lot larger than mine."

"If you keep stimulating it like *that*, it will get even bigger."

"Yes," Clover smiled, feeling the nub growing as she rolled her fingers over it.

"That feels good," Lori grunted, gyrating her hips as Clover slipped another finger inside to palpate the bulb.

Suddenly, Clover felt the organ expanding outwards like a growing penis, until it popped out of Lori's slit, undulating like a worm.

"What the–" she said, pulling back in surprise.

"Don't worry," Lori smiled. "We're just built a little differently than you humans. But our sexual organs work in much the same way, and feel similar. Don't be shy about touching me and experimenting with different techniques. We're still getting to know one another..."

Clover paused for a moment to inspect the throbbing pink appendage, then she lowered her hand to pinch it softly between her thumb and forefinger, rolling it softly between her fingers.

"Yes," Lori groaned. "Just like that."

"It's almost feels like a boy's *cock*," Clover said, staring at the unusually shaped gland with wide eyes. "Why does it stick outside your body when you're aroused?"

"I'm not sure," Lori said, pinching her nipples while Clover played with her flapping organ. "Maybe it's because we can't separate our legs like you humans can and we need to find other ways to stimulate ourselves. There are plenty of underwater objects to rub our bodies onto."

"Like other mermaids?" Clover smiled, stroking Lori's cocklet slowly up and down.

"Sometimes," Lori grunted. "Or sometimes, we just like to stimulate ourselves against a soft piece of coral. Our fleshy projections show the mermen when we're receptive and fertile."

Clover lowered her head closer to Lori's twitching organ, fascinated by its strange and erotic shape.

"Do the mermen and mermaids also like to *suck* on it like this?" she said, encircling Lori's gland with her lips, sucking on it like a man's cock.

"Yes," Lori moaned. "Although you seem to have had a little more *practice* than some of the others."

"I won't lie," Clover smiled as she slurped on Lori's twitching appendage. "I like to lick both men and women. But I've never been with a woman with such a large clitoris before. Or penis, or whatever you call it."

"We call it our jin," Lori panted, thrusting her hips more rapidly into Clover's mouth. "I think you humans call this characteristic *androgynous*. We have the ability to reproduce both as males and females."

"No way!" Clover said, suddenly sitting up. "This thing can squirt *semen* too?"

"If that's what you call your reproductive seed," Lori nodded.

"Oh my God," Clover gushed. "In that case, do you mind if I stimulate it a different way? I'm getting insanely turned on touching you, and I'd love to feel you inside me."

"I was wondering what was taking you so long," Lori smiled. "I've been dying to watch you ride my other side ever since you felt me up on the trip to our lagoon.

"Mmm," Clover smiled. "Allow me feel you up a different way..."

She raised her hips a little higher and shifted her body a few inches up Lori's body, then lowered her dripping pussy over Lori's twitching nub until she felt her clit pressing against her scaly stomach.

"Wow," Clover grunted. "I've never been fucked by a woman before. At least not like this."

"You're not disappointed my jin isn't as big as *Jessop's*?" Lori said.

"Are you kidding me?" Clover panted, rocking her hips harder over Lori's scaly skin. "This is way hotter than having sex with a man. Your bumpy skin stimulates my clit in a way

I've never experienced before. And I've never known a man with such pretty *tits*..."

As Clover leaned forward to suck Lori's nipples while she rocked over her stiffening knob, Lori threw her head back, flapping her tail softly against Clover's ass.

"Mmm," Clover grunted, enjoying the sensation of being spanked while she fucked Lori's twitching dick. "Does that feel good? Am I stimulating you the way you like it?"

"No one's ever done it to me like this before," Lori panted, pulling Clover's face down so they could kiss while they ground their hips together. "Fuck me with your pretty pussy, Clover. I'm going to spray my *agua* inside you soon..."

"Yes, baby," Clover moaned into Lori's mouth. "I want to feel you coming inside me. You feel incredible."

As Lori clamped her arms tighter around Clover's back, she began pumping her hips faster against her pussy while her tail slapped harder against her ass. When she moaned deeply into Clover's mouth and Clover realized she was climaxing, Clover quickly lost control of her own rapidly escalating pleasure, squirting long and hard over Lori's spasming slit.

"Lorelei," Clover grunted, her chest heaving overtop her new friend as they reveled in the afterglow of their mutual climax. "That's the most incredible experience I've ever had. What other surprises are you and your mysterious people keeping from us?"

"Well, you haven't had sex with the *mermen* yet," she smiled. "Something tells me Jessop might be having his eyes opened in an entirely different kind of way on the other side of the island..."

6

———

A couple of hundred feet toward the other side of the island, Jessop and Caol were arguing over who should sleep where.

"That's very kind of you to offer this last available swing for me to sleep on," Jessop said. "But you must be exhausted from your long swim over from the mainland. I'm happy to sleep on the beach if you're used to sleeping in the hammock."

"I can sleep pretty much anywhere," Caol said. "You're our guest, and I'm sure you're accustomed to sleeping on something more comfortable than the sand."

"We seem to have reached a stalemate," Jessop smiled. "Why don't we arm wrestle to decide?"

Caol raised his eyebrows in surprise, peering at Jessop's smaller build and thinner arms, then he glanced at the bulge in his pants between his legs.

"I'm not sure it will be a fair contest," Caol said, lying down on the sand next to the hammock. "But if you think you can beat me, I'm game."

Jessop lay down facing Caol and extended his arm,

bending it at the elbow. When they clasped hands, he felt a bolt of electricity coursing through his veins as he smiled at Caol's handsome face.

"Are you ready?" he said. "On the count of three. Three, two, one, go–!"

As the two men tensed their shoulder and arm muscles, they peered at one another, grunting softly. Caol was surprised how well Jessop could hold his ground against his superior strength, and Jessop wondered if he still carried some residual super-powers from his encounter with the mage at the Cock and Hen bar.

After a few minutes of tipping back and forth, Caol released his grip and grinned.

"It looks like a tie," he said. "I think the only fair solution is for us to *share* the hammock."

Jessop cocked his head, peering at Caol in surprise.

"You think there's room for *both* of us on there?" he said.

"It's been done before," Caol smiled. "The strings and matting are strong enough to support two people, and it's roomier than you might imagine."

"Okay..." Jessop said, rolling his hands warily over the woven matting. "Who should go first?"

"I'm a little heavier than you, so why don't I lie down first? That way, you'll be able to find a position that's most comfortable for you."

Caol placed his hands on the side of the hammock, then deftly raised himself onto the swing, lying flat on his back with his hands behind his head. Jessop peered at his long, marine figure, then delicately raised himself up, nestling in gently beside him. The hammock swung slowly over the sand, but it held their weight and Jessop pinched his brows, feeling the strange sensation of Caol's scaly skin touching his hips.

"Do you sleep with other mermaids here often?" Jessop said.

"And *mermen*," Caol smiled.

"So you like both males and females?"

"We don't limit ourselves to who we wish to sleep or have sex with," Caol grinned, twisting his tail seductively. "That seems to be more of a *human* proclivity."

"Actually," Jessop said, feeling his pants growing tighter as his cock swelled in the tight confinement. "There are plenty of humans that like it both ways."

"How about *you*?" Caol said. "I noticed you spent a fair amount of time eyeing up Lori's tits on the beach earlier."

"She's very beautiful," Jessop nodded. "I'm just not used to seeing a woman baring her breasts like that in public."

"And yet I felt your penis becoming aroused while you rode my back on the way over to our lagoon?"

"Well, to be fair, your ass was rocking up and down against it for almost an hour..."

"Do you *like* my fish-shaped ass?" Caol smiled, tracing his fingers down Jessop's arm.

"It's certainly different from what I'm used to," Jessop said. "How exactly do you mermaids and mermen manage to have sex, with everything hidden out of the way?"

"They don't stay hidden *all* the time," Caol, said, peering down toward the slit in his midsection. "See for yourself."

Jessop traced his gaze below Caol's navel and his eyes suddenly widened when he saw the merman's pink phallus pushing out of his slit. It was shaped differently than his own, wide and thick, with a flattened shape more akin to a tongue than a penis.

"It's shaped so different from mine," he said. "And it moves like a *worm*."

"Or an eel," Caol chuckled, noticing Jessop's captivated

expression. "It makes it easier to slide around the inside of our mermaid's vagina. Go ahead and touch it if you'd like."

Jessop reached his hand out slowly to touch the tip of the organ, and it suddenly twitched.

"Does it feel good when you touch it?" he said.

"Yes," Caol nodded. "Even more when someone *else* touches it."

"How do you stimulate it?"

"In much the same way I imagine you stimulate *yours*," Caol smiled. "By rubbing it in various places..."

Jessop lowered his hand over the phallus, wrapping his fingers around the slippery flesh and rubbing it up and down.

"Yes," Caol groaned. "Kind of like that."

As Jessop moved his hand further down the instrument, he watched in fascination as it squirmed and writhed in his hands.

"Wow," he said, growing more aroused by the moment while he caressed Caol's organ. "The mermaids must really enjoy all the ways this thing can move inside them. It seems a lot more versatile than my penis."

"Why don't you take off your clothes and compare?" Caol said. "I'm just as intrigued to see what a *human* cock looks like."

"Now that you mention it," Jessop said, squirming on the hammock beside Caol. "They are feeling a bit constraining right about now..."

He sat up and quickly removed his pants and shirt, throwing them onto the ground beside the hammock.

Caol reached down and encircled his erection in his webbed hands, rolling his thumb over Jessop's bulbous crown.

"It's a little smaller than mine," he smiled, feeling a drop of pre-cum sliding out of Jessop's tip. "But it's just as warm and slippery. Can you move up a little higher so I can take a closer look?"

Jessop angled his thigh over Caol's stomach and shifted his hips higher over his hairy chest, feeling his balls tingling as his dick flapped excitedly onto his stomach.

"It's a little firmer than mine," Caol said, gripping Jessop's hard dick with his right hand as he caressed his testicles with the other. "But what are these strange round objects at the base of it?"

"They're my testicles," Jessop chuckled. "Where I produce semen to impregnate our women."

"Does it feel good when I touch you there *too*?" Caol said.

"Yes," Jessop panted, watching the tip of his dick twitching a few inches away from Caol's square jaw.

"What about when I *lick* it?" Caol said, tilting his head forward to engulf Jessop's tool in his mouth.

"Fuck, yes," Jessop panted, watching the merman sucking his dick as he fondled his balls.

Suddenly he felt something slithering up the crack of his ass, and his eyes widened when he realized it was Caol's penis growing even longer.

"Holy *shit*, Caol," Jessop grunted. "How big does that thing get?"

"The more excited I am, the bigger it gets," Caol smiled, popping Jessop's dick in and out of his mouth. "Do you like having your anus stimulated at the same time?"

"Not normally," Jessop said. "But your dick feels more like a tongue. And it's very sensitive down there..."

"How about if I press it *inside*?" Caol said, pushing his mouth all the way down over Jessop's cock.

"Fuck yes," Jessop panted, closing his eyes in ecstasy from the simultaneous stimulation to his penis, balls, and butthole. "Fuck me with your slippery eel. I've never been stimulated in all three places at the same time."

"Mmmft," Caol grunted, pressing his organ deeper into Jessop's anus.

Jessop could feel it conforming to the contours of his rectum, and the sensation of it slithering inside him felt more erotic than anything he'd ever experienced.

"Oh my God," Jessop growled, rolling his ass over Caol's twitching organ. "This is insane. I had no idea you mer-people were so versatile."

"We're just getting started," Caol smiled, temporarily popping Jessop's dick out of his mouth as he glanced up at him. "That slit serves two purposes. We can fuck each other *both* ways. When you're finished here, I can't wait for you to probe *me* inside also."

"*What?*" Jessop said, bulging his eyes as he watched Caol bobbing his head up and down his prick while he slithered his organ deeper inside his hole. "You're going to make me come. Oh *fuckkk...*"

7

———

The following morning, Clover, Tara, and Jessop wandered down to the shore with their new friends, where a group of mermaids were busily preparing breakfast on the beach. They didn't even bother putting their clothes back on, feeling self-conscious mingling with the others in their natural skin.

"Come join us for something to eat," Ronan said, motioning for them to sit with the group assembled in a large circle around a communal serving platter.

"What are you preparing?" Tara said, pausing to appraise the spread as everybody stared at her furry crotch.

"Fresh sea bass and chopped coconut," Lori said, kneeling down next to Clover, clasping her hand.

She reached onto the flat driftwood, scooping up a handful of dripping fish and fruit.

"Should we just help ourselves with our *fingers*?" Jessop said.

"Absolutely," Caol grinned. "There's a reason the gods bestowed us with hands."

The three friends reached out and pulled some morsels

off the tray, and when they placed the food in their mouths, their eyes widened in surprise.

"Wow," Clover gasped. "This is the best sushi I've ever had. Talk about farm to table..."

"Sushi?" Ronan said, scrunching his forehead. "Farm to what–"

"That's what we call uncooked fish where I come from," Clover chuckled. "Farm to table simply means the food is eaten shortly after it's harvested. And this is by far the freshest fish I've ever tasted."

"And the coconut juice gives it a sweet taste," Tara nodded.

"I'm just happy to be eating something besides wild boar or rabbit for a change," Jessop chuckled.

Everybody paused for a moment, peering between the human's legs at their exposed genitals.

"So how did everybody sleep last night?" Lori said, breaking the awkward silence. "Did you find the hammocks as comfortable as your usual sleeping arrangements?"

"Even more so," Tara said, turning to smile at Ronan. "Though it took a little getting used to the constant movement."

"Movement isn't *always* bad," Clover said, squeezing Lori's hand. "Especially when you've got a pretty girl lying beside you."

"What about you, Jessop?" Tara said, noticing her friend being suspiciously silent sitting next to Caol, who was nibbling his food with a strange grin on his face.

"I didn't have a pretty girl lying next to me," he smiled. "But there was plenty of swinging going on..."

"Speaking of *exercise*," Ronan interjected. "Why don't we all go for a swim in the lagoon after breakfast? The tide is low and the top of the reef is exposed above the water. This is my favorite time, when all the colorful sea creatures are crowded into our little pool."

"Sounds like a dream," Clover nodded. "I had so much fun playing with the sea lions yesterday. What other kinds of animals live here?"

"Just about everything you can imagine," he smiled. "Clown fish, striped bass, manta rays, porpoises, even dolphins sometimes."

"What about *sharks*?" Jessop said, his ears perking up suddenly.

"They're pretty rare," Ronan nodded. "But when we do get an occasional stray, they're usually pretty small and harmless nurse sharks. With our superior numbers, they don't often come into our sheltered bay."

"I'm up for a swim if you guys are," Clover said, jumping up excitedly. She pranced up to the edge of the shore then splashed into the water noisily. "Come on, the water's warm as soup!"

Tara and Jessop followed soon after and before long, the entire band of mermaids and mermen were swimming playfully in the crystal-clear water, rubbing up against one another while flashing their aroused genitals. Clover noticed they didn't seem to have a preference as to who they mated with, with the mermaids equally interested rubbing up against the females as the mermen were with the males. Even Jessop seemed excited swimming between both sexes, inserting his wagging pecker into any hole that presented itself.

After a while, Clover became separated from her new friend as she stared at the wondrous sight of the abundant sea creatures darting in and out of the luminescent coral. Suddenly, she noticed some churning water near the opening to the lagoon and she lifted her head above the water, hearing some loud squealing. Peering in the direction of the gap, she saw a huge gray animal breaching above the surface as it tossed a frightened seal pup high in the air.

"Shark!" Ronan bellowed, suddenly thrusting his head above the water.

"What?" Clover said, peering at him with wide eyes. "But you said–"

"It's a *great white!*" he said. "And a large one. Everybody needs to get out of the lagoon now!"

As all the mermaids and merman began flapping toward the shore, Clover glanced up, watching the seal's separated body spraying blood all over the clear surface of the lagoon. Moments later, she heard a more terrifying scream, and as she turned in the direction of the noise, she saw a mermaid lying face down on the surface of the water while a huge fin circled slowly around it. The waves from the shark's movement rolled the body onto its side, and when she recognized Lori's blond hair and pretty face, she gasped.

"Lorelei!" Clover yelled, flapping madly in the direction of her stricken friend.

Suddenly she felt the powerful arms of Ronan scoop her up as he steered her toward the shore. When he deposited her onto the sand, she peered at him with desperate eyes.

"Save Lori!" she yelled, glancing at the widening circle of blood around her body. "She needs my help far more than me."

"We will," he said as the other mermen assembled around their leader. "You stay here with the others and keep out of the water."

Clover glanced around her, noticing Tara and Jessop looking equally terrified, and as she crawled up next to them, they bundled together, clasping their arms around one another.

"Oh my God," Tara gasped, watching the mermen forming a protective ring around the drifting mermaid. "Is that *Lori?*"

"Yes," Clover said, her body still shaking in shock. "And she's badly hurt."

"Look at the size of that thing," Jessop said, watching the enormous shark dipping its body in and out of the water as the mermen tried to scare it away. "It must be at least twenty-five-feet long. They better get her out of there before he gobbles up the rest of them."

While the mermen flapped their tails angrily at the circling animal, they gradually steered Lori's body onto shore, where another group of mermaids pulled her up onto the sand. The three friends rushed over and their mouths fell open when they saw a three-foot wide gash over the side of Lori's hips. She was bleeding heavily onto the sand and wincing in pain.

"You're *alive!*" Clover said, kneeling down beside her and cradling her head.

"Not for long," Lori said, raising her head to glance at her wound. "I've seen this kind of injury before. I'll soon lose all my vital fluid. Hold me, Clover..."

Clover peered up at Tara, remembering how she'd nursed their dragons back to health.

"Can't you do something?" she asked.

Tara paused for a moment as she watched the mermaids holding palm leaves and spreading coconut oil over the gash.

"The wound is too large," she said. "It has to be closed before she bleeds out. Try to compress the wound until I get back with some needle and thread..."

As she dashed off to the section of the island where she'd left her belongings, Ronan flipped out of the water with the rest of the mermen, watching the shark continuing to circulate around the lagoon.

"Needle and thread?" he said, peering at Lori with a puzzled expression.

"She might be able to close the wound," Clover nodded as she cradled Lori's head, peering into her thinning eyes. "She's had some experience with this sort of thing."

When Tara returned with her first-aid kit, the mermaids pulled away from the side of Lori's body while the elf kneeled on the sand next to her.

"Try to keep her still," Tara said, glancing up at the mermen looking on in shock. "This is going to be hard enough without her writhing in agony."

Ronan and Caol shifted over to the other side of Tara and placed their hands over Lori's shaking knees and hips to hold her still.

"You're *hurt!*" Jessop said, suddenly noticing a big chunk taken out of Caol's tail.

"I'll be fine," Caol said, more concerned with Lori's condition. "It's just a flesh wound. Let's take care of Lorelei first."

Tara glanced up to peer at his wound then quickly set back to work patching Lori up.

"I'll tend to you when I'm done here," she said. "But this could very well use up all my thread. Her wound is deep and severe."

"Can you save her?" Clover said, looking up at her friend with pleading eyes.

"It's going to be close," Tara said, winding her needle through Lori's gaping flesh and slowly closing the tear. "Try to keep her calm. The lower her blood pressure, the better."

As Clover ran her hands softly through Lori's hair and caressed her face, the rest of the group looked on in silence while they watched Tara work her magic. Twenty minutes later, she sat back and exhaled deeply, staring at her handiwork.

"It's not pretty, but if she survives the night, she should live. Right now, she needs rest and plenty of fluids."

"I don't think we should move her right now," Ronan said, leaning back to examine the sawtooth pattern of laces over Lori's scaly skin. "Let's keep her here on the beach until she regains her strength."

Some mermaids returned from the forest with fresh water, and as Clover held up her head, Caol tilted a hollowed-out coconut shell over her lips.

"Here, baby," he said. "Try to drink. Stay with us."

As he kneeled beside the stricken mermaid, Tara glanced at his injured tail.

"Let me take a look at that," she said, moving behind his flanks. "It doesn't look too bad. The shark only chomped off the cartilage near the tip. There's no blood loss, so you should be okay."

Caol glanced over his shoulder, wincing at his half-eaten tail.

"If you call being half the man I *used* to be okay," he grimaced.

"At least you kept the important parts," Jessop smiled. "The half-*man* part of you still appears to be fully functional."

"What about the *shark*?" Tara said, noticing the giant animal still slithering menacingly around the perimeter of the island, chasing the remaining fish into hiding places around the coral.

"We'll just have to wait it out until he leaves," Ronan said. "He's far too large for us to neutralize. Unfortunately, we'll have to stay on safe ground until he's filled his belly."

8

———

After Lori was stabilized and placed under close supervision, the rest of the tribe watched in horror as the great white shark circled the lagoon terrorizing the trapped animals, tossing juvenile sea lions and seals in the air like popcorn.

"Why is he *throwing* them like that?" Jessop asked Ronan and Caol. "With his size, he could just swallow them whole."

"It's a strange predilection with these creatures," Caol said. "They seem to enjoy tormenting them before finishing them off. It's like it's some kind of *game* for them."

"Isn't there anything you can do?" Tara said, wincing as she listened to the screams of the frightened animals. "He's picking them off one by one."

"Unfortunately, no," Ronan said, shaking his head. "There's a reason they're called apex predators. With his superior size and swimming ability, we're simply no threat to him."

"Even with a hundred of you, and only *one* of him?" Jessop said.

"Our hands are no match for his powerful jaws," Ronan

nodded. "We don't have anything equivalent to attack him with."

"What about my *arrows*?" Tara said. "At least I might be able to slow him down a little..."

"The arrows wouldn't be much good underwater," Ronan said. "As long as he stays some distance from the shore and partially submerged, I'm afraid they wouldn't have much effect."

Jessop watched the circling beast, shaking his head at its seeming impunity attacking and eating any animal that ventured out of its hiding place.

"What if we trapped it inside the lagoon?" he said.

"Are you *crazy?*" Caol said. "Why would we want to do that? We're trying to get it out of here, not keep it caged up like some kind of theme park attraction."

"But if you let it go, you'll just be encouraging it to return anytime it wants to continue terrorizing your secluded sanctuary."

"What exactly did you have in mind?" Ronan said, intrigued with Jessop's proposal. "How would we trap such a large animal?"

Jessop glanced around the perimeter of the lagoon, watching the sea waves crashing against the raised coral reef encircling the island.

"You said the island is protected when there's a low tide by the raised reef encircling the island. During that period, there's only one way in and out of the lagoon, through the narrow opening in the coral on the west side. What if we somehow *blocked* the gap so the shark couldn't escape? Sooner or later, he'd run out of food...."

"And *then* what?" Caol said. "He'd be even more danger-ous, desperate to attack anything that came within striking distance."

Tara nodded at her friend, impressed with his ingenious idea.

"We could lure him into the shallows," she said. "Then I could slow him down with my arrows, much like a bull-fighter does with his pointers before dealing the final blow."

"And what would be our final blow?" Ronan said.

"I'm still figuring that one out," Tara said. "But with the shark injured and incapacitated, presumably it would only be a matter of time before he bled out or starved to death."

"You're missing one important ingredient in this brilliant plan," Caol said. "The tide rises and falls every twelve hours. We'd only have a short period of time to catch him before he could escape over the submerged coral during high tide."

"That should be enough time to neutralize him with all the resources at our disposal," Jessop said.

"How do you propose to close the opening?" Ronan said. "Even at low tide, the gap is almost twelve feet deep. It would take us days to fill it with rocks, during which time he'd just escape over the submerged reef."

"Not if we block it with your hardy *swings*," Tara smiled. "You showed me yourself how strong they are. If you stacked them one over the other then tied them together around the edges of the coral, do you think that might keep him in long enough for us to turn the tables?"

"It's one thing to support two people sleeping on the cot," Caol scoffed. "And quite another to stop a ten-thousand-pound *shark*."

Ronan paused for a moment, considering the humans' plan.

"It's a possibility," he nodded, turning to Caol. "Have you got any better ideas? How many more of our people are we willing to let it mutilate before we take matters into our own hands?"

Caol glanced at his friends then looked up into the sky, noticing the sun arcing overhead.

"We better get started soon then," he said. "If we're going to have enough time to set the trap."

R onan mustered the rest of the mermen while they hacked down the hammocks from the surrounding trees, then a group assembled around the opening to the lagoon, watching the shark gliding warily nearby.

"How are we going to get down there long enough to tie the material around the coral with the shark getting up this close?" Caol said.

Clover paused for a moment, having rejoined the group after Lori fell asleep, recovering from her wounds.

"Why don't you throw some *chum* into the water at the other end of the lagoon?" she said.

"Chum?" Caol said, peering at her with a puzzled expression.

"It's chunks of freshly caught fish," Clover said. "It least it worked in all the shark movies I've seen."

"She's right," Ronan nodded. "Sharks have a superior sense of smell. They can smell an injured animal from miles away. Can you ask the women to prepare the food and drop it in the water on the other side of the island where the lagoon shallows? Hopefully that will buy us enough time to block the hole."

"I'll go with her," Tara nodded. "Maybe I can distract him a little longer with a few well-placed arrows."

"Okay," Ronan nodded, watching the waves beginning to wash up over the crest of the reef. "But hurry, we've only got a few hours left before the sea level rises above the top of the coral."

After the women prepared the bait and retreated to the other side of the island, it didn't take long for the shark to pick up the scent of the blood in the water and turn in their direction.

"Let's go," Ronan said to the other mermen holding onto the ends of the hammocks. "Each of you take an end and tie the cords tightly around the exposed sections of the coral. We might only have a few minutes before the shark returns."

He turned to Caol, placing his hand over his shoulder.

"With your injury, it's best you act as our lookout. I don't want you in the water when that thing comes back looking for the easiest pickings."

As the rest of the mermen dived into the water and began tying the hammocks end-over-end to block the opening, Caol and Jessop stood a few feet above them on the promontory, watching the men working below.

"Do you think this will work?" Jessop said, holding his sword protectively at his side.

"There's as good a chance as *any*," Caol nodded, scanning the lagoon for any sign of the returning shark. "But I don't think that blade of yours is going to be much help against that thing. Besides the fact that you swim a lot slower than him, you wouldn't be able to swing your sword fast enough under the water to do much good."

"Maybe so," Jessop said. "All the same, it makes me feel a little safer having it by my side. This thing has saved my hide more times than I care to remember."

Back on the other side of the island, Clover, Tara, and the rest of the mermaids lifted handfuls of chopped seafood on driftwood trays until they reached a sheltered bay with shallow water.

"This looks like as good a spot as any," Tara said, peering at the steep embankments surrounding the bay. "I'll be able to get into position to fire my arrows at him while he's feeding on the chum. Hopefully, we can injure him enough for the rest of the mermen to finish him off."

"Is there anything I can do to help?" Clover said, watching the mermaids waiting for their signal to proceed.

"Just keep a lookout for now," Tara nodded. "I'll need you to signal the rest of the group when the shark decides he's had his fill."

"Okay," Clover said, nodding for the mermaids to wade into the shallow water to spread the chum over the surface.

As they did so, Tara circled around to the highest point on the bank, placing an arrow on her bowstring and pulling the cord back, preparing to fire. After the women finished spreading the fish meat, they returned to the safety of the shore, waiting for the shark to take the bait. But after a few minutes, there was no sign of the animal, and Clover peered up at Tara nervously.

"Do you think he can smell the fish from this far away?" Clover said.

"I don't know," Tara said. "You seem to be the shark expert around here. What do your fairy tales say?"

Clover paused for a moment, remembering one of the scenes from her favorite shark movie, *Jaws*. In the scene where the injured boat captain was in the shark's sights, the police chief splashed the water and yelled to distract the shark in another direction.

"I'm not sure if this will work," she smiled. "But I've heard sharks also respond to unusual sounds and movement in the water, like it's an injured animal. Let me go in a little distance and make a commotion to see if we can attract his attention this way."

"Alright," Tara said, but don't go in too far. "And make sure you get the hell out of there as soon as I see him coming around the bend."

Clover nodded, then waded a few feet into the water until she was submerged hip-deep. Then she slapped her hands rapidly over the surface, yelling loudly.

"Help!" she screamed, mimicking the sound and appearance of Lori who'd been attacked earlier. "I'm drowning! I'm injured and I can't move!"

Tara shook her head, chuckling temporarily at her friend's exaggerated histrionics, then she noticed the large grey animal snaking around the bend in the lagoon.

"Get out now!" she yelled to Clover. "It's coming!"

Clover peered in the direction of the bend, seeing the giant fin heading straight toward her while she struggled to march back onto shore with her legs feeling like molasses under the heavy surf. As the shark picked up his pace, undulating rapidly through the water in Clover's direction, Tara began flinging arrows from her quiver, striking the beast on its flanks. The shark turned suddenly, unsure what was attacking it as it gobbled up the chum while Clover scrambled back onto the beach.

"Keep shooting that fucker!" Clover yelled at Tara while she continued flinging arrows into its side.

But the shallow jabs just seemed to aggravate the animal even more as it thrashed and meandered wildly in the shallow water. After Tara had run out of arrows, snaring it with only half her allotment, the shark peered up at the elf with a hooded eye, then it flapped back out of the bay in the direction of the lagoon opening.

"It's coming back!" Clover screamed, cupping her hands over her mouth to project her voice as much as possible to warn the mermen of the approaching threat.

When Jessop heard the commotion from the other side of the island, he leaned down and swiped his sword over the surface of the water to warn the submerged mermen to return to the surface. While the injured shark swam angrily through the middle of the lagoon in their direction, they scrambled out of the water onto the top of the reef just in time. As the shark butted the netting with its pointed head, Caol peered down, noticing large holes in the mesh.

"It's not going to hold!" he shouted to his friends.

As the mermen shook their heads realizing the barrier was about to collapse and the shark circled back to take one more run at the disintegrating barricade, Caol turned to Ronan and nodded.

"I'm going to try to distract it while you repair the netting," he said, suddenly jumping off the pier into the water, swimming in the opposite direction of the approaching shark.

"No, *wait*–!" Ronan yelled, trying to stop his friend from the suicide mission.

But it was too late. As Caol swam through the water at half his normal speed with his damaged fin, the shark circled around to chase after him. When he realized that he was cornered and had nowhere to escape, he turned back around, making a beeline to the narrow opening in the netting, hoping to slip through before the larger shark got held up.

While everybody looked on in horror at the sight of the enormous animal closing the gap with the flapping merman, Jessop set his feet firmly against the stubby coral surface, raising his sword above his head with two hands. He had no idea what he could do to save Caol, but he was determined not to let the shark take another chunk out of his friend. As Caol swam underneath him and slipped through the narrow opening in the barrier, Jessop suddenly leaped into the air, screaming like a wildcat.

When the huge beast reached the disintegrating wall, Jessop dived into the water a few inches above its head, driving the tip of his sword deep into the shark's skull. With a huge pool of blood forming around the injured animal, all the mermen peered down into the murky water wondering whose blood it was. With no sign of Jessop returning to the surface, they feared the worst, and as Caol scrambled back up onto the rocks looking on with his friends, he turned to Ronan, shaking his head.

"Where's Jessop?" he said. "What happened to the shark?"

"He jumped into the water to spear it when he saw you were about to get bitten," Ronan said.

"He *what?*" Caol said, hardly believing Jessop would do such a foolhardy thing. "Why would he do that–?"

Suddenly, Jessop popped his head above the water and clamored atop of the motionless shark, pulling his sword out of its head, jabbing it repeatedly with wild eyes.

"I think it's dead, Jessop," Caol chuckled, amused by the fury at which he continued attacking the animal. "It looks like you saved the day, not to mention my hide."

"That's good," Jessop grinned, peering up as he rolled gently atop the floating carcass. "Because I hadn't quite finished *exploring* your hide. Help me out of here while I make sure I've still got all my man parts."

9

———

For the next few days, the three friends remained on the island while Lori made a slow recovery, helping the mermen create a stronger barrier for the gap in their lagoon to keep unwanted visitors out. At nighttime, everyone returned to their previous pairings, resuming their playful activities on the rebuilt hammocks, growing more attached to their unlikely partners with each passing day.

"What are your plans now that everything's back to normal?" Lori asked, cuddling up next to Clover on their gently swinging cot. "Why don't you stay with us a little longer? We could use an extra pair of hands, not to mention legs, around here. Plus you humans seem to have some extra talents to keep us out of trouble."

"I don't know," Clover said, running her fingers softly over Lori's rapidly healing scar. "I don't think we belong in a place like this. It's like the mythical place Atlantis, where sea creatures live protected and far removed from the destructive habits of humans. You deserve to enjoy your secluded paradise in peace. It's the perfect sanctuary for your kind."

Lori smiled, rolling over to kiss Clover gently.

"Well, I'm going to miss some of your special talents..."

"I'm just glad that shark missed your important parts when he took a bite out of you," Clover said, slipping her finger into Lori's dripping slit while they kissed. "At least everything seems to be working like it was before."

"Yes," Lori cooed, pressing her flaring gland out of her hole. "And I see you haven't lost your touch knowing how to excite me."

"Mmm," Clover smiled, rolling gently overtop of Lori while slipping her clit into her pussy. "I'm going to miss feeling you inside me after I'm gone..."

O n the other side of the island, Jessop and Caol were experiencing their own kind of entertainment on their rustling hammock.

"That was quite a dangerous feat you undertook, going after that huge shark in his own element," Caol said, caressing Jessop's balls as his penis began to rise up over his stomach.

"Well, I couldn't very well let him swallow you up before I finished having my way with you," Jessop said, rubbing his hard-on against the underside of Caol's lengthening phallus.

"Oh?" Caol said, humping his hips against Jessop as they frotted their organs together. "Have you been dreaming about fucking me like I did to you on our first night together?"

"It only seems fair," Jessop grinned, raising up on his knees to point the tip of his cock into Caol's slit. "I'm accustomed to being the one *giving* the pounding, not taking it."

"Mmm," Caol grunted as Jessop sunk his tool deep into

his hole. "You might not be quite as big as the other mermen, but you're just as much of a man. Fuck me with that hard dick of yours and let me feel you coming inside me."

"Ungh," Jessop groaned, feeling Caol's thick organ sliding against his belly as he slapped his tightening balls against the merman's scaly hips. "But what happens if I deposit my seed inside you?"

"Let's just say this might not be the last time a human body part crawls out of my hole," Caol smiled.

A few hundred yards to the west, Tara and Ronan also lay in their hammock, reminiscing while they kissed and caressed one another.

"That took a lot of courage for you to go back into the lagoon with that big shark still swimming around," she said, twirling her fingers through his chest hair.

"Not to mention for you and Clover to keep it distracted long enough for us to trap it in the lagoon," Ronan said.

"Jessop was the real hero of the day," she said, sliding her hand down his belly toward his widening slit.

"Will you be resuming your usual ways with him when you leave here?"

"It's going to take some getting used to his smaller cock," she grinned, grasping Ronan's lengthening tool with her hand. "But I suppose he'll have to do in a pinch."

"Are you elves always so resourceful?" he grunted as Tara began sliding her hand over his thick appendage. "Besides your impressive archery skills, I had no idea you were such a good seamstress."

"Only the *female* elves," Tara grinned. "The men are usually only good for one thing."

"Let me guess," Ronan said, rolling overtop of Tara to insert his big organ between her splayed legs. "Creating lots and lots of tadpoles?"

"Something like that..." Tara smiled, pulling Ronan's face down to hers while she kissed him as their bodies melded together.

R eady for more erotic chills and thrills? Order the next exciting volume in Clover's Fantasy Adventures:

Never trust a witch who only wants one thing from you...

ALSO BY VICTORIA RUSH

Wet your whistle a hundred different ways with Jade's Erotic Adventures. Browse the full collection of Victoria Rush steamy stories here:

Click to scan your favorites...

FOLLOW VICTORIA RUSH:

Want to keep informed of my latest erotic book releases? Sign up for my newsletter and receive a FREE bonus book:

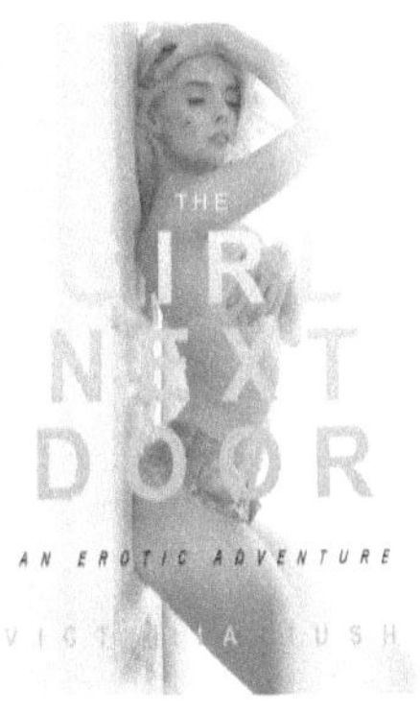

Spying on the neighbors just got a lot more interesting...

9 781990 118722